SANTA DUCK

DAVID MILGRIM

G. P. PUTNAM'S SONS

For Wyatt, the greatest guy in the
world, galaxy, and universe.

G. P. PUTNAM'S SONS
A division of Penguin Young Readers Group.
Published by The Penguin Group.
Penguin Group (USA) Inc., 375 Hudson Street, New York, NY 10014, U.S.A.
Penguin Group (Canada), 90 Eglinton Avenue East, Suite 700, Toronto,
Ontario M4P 2Y3, Canada (a division of Pearson Penguin Canada Inc.).
Penguin Books Ltd, 80 Strand, London WC2R 0RL, England.
Penguin Ireland, 25 St. Stephen's Green, Dublin 2, Ireland (a division of Penguin Books Ltd.).
Penguin Group (Australia), 250 Camberwell Road, Camberwell, Victoria 3124, Australia
(a division of Pearson Australia Group Pty Ltd).
Penguin Books India Pvt Ltd, 11 Community Centre, Panchsheel Park, New Delhi - 110 017, India.
Penguin Group (NZ), 67 Apollo Drive, Rosedale, North Shore 0632, New Zealand
(a division of Pearson New Zealand Ltd).
Penguin Books (South Africa) (Pty) Ltd, 24 Sturdee Avenue, Rosebank,
Johannesburg 2196, South Africa.
Penguin Books Ltd, Registered Offices: 80 Strand, London WC2R 0RL, England.

Published simultaneously in Canada. Manufactured in China by South China Printing Co. Ltd.
Design by Marikka Tamura. Text set in Administer Bold.
The art was done in digital ink and digital oil pastel.
Library of Congress Cataloging-in-Publication Data
Milgrim, David. Santa Duck / David Milgrim.   p. cm.
Summary: When Nicholas Duck, wearing a Santa hat and coat he found
on his doorstep, goes looking for Santa to tell him what he wants for Christmas,
all the other animals mistake him for Mr. Claus. 1. Santa Claus—Juvenile fiction.
[1. Santa Claus—Fiction. 2. Ducks—Fiction. 3. Animals—Fiction.
4. Christmas—Fiction. 5. Humorous stories.]
I. Title. PZ7.M5955San 2008 [E]—dc22 2007043162
ISBN 978-0-399-25018-7
3 5 7 9 10 8 6 4 2

Nicholas Duck had only one day left to find Santa. "If I don't tell him what I want," he quacked, "it's going to be another year of socks and underwear."

On his way out, Nicholas found a surprise.

It was a cozy, warm coat and
a genuine, official Santa hat!

Nicholas had no idea who had
given it to him, but he liked it.

Then Nicholas met a chicken.
"Santa Duck!" the chicken said.
"I've been looking for you
everywhere!"

After that he
met a cat.

I want a mouse and a Canary and a trout and maybe a couple of nice, plump hamsters.
Better bring some egg nog too.

Then he met a turtle.

And a really, really fast race car that goes really, really fast, and a helmet with goggles and flames painted on the side!
Look, it's Santa!
COOL!

And a squirrel.

And a rabbit.

Nicholas couldn't figure out WHAT
was going on. All he could do was
scratch his head. When he did, his
hat fell off. "Of course!" he said.
"It must be the hat!"

So Nicholas gave
it to a cow.

The cow was very happy with her new hat.
Nicholas was even happier to be rid of it.

Nicholas continued on his merry search once again.

Then came two kangaroos, a pig,
a mouse, a goat, and Nicholas's
own kid brother!

Nicholas started
running and running
and running.

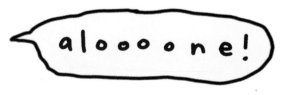

Until he ran into
Santa himself.

Santa asked Nicholas what everyone wanted, and Nicholas told him.

After they said good night,
Nicholas realized he had forgotten
to tell Santa his own list!

But it was too late!

Then, when Nicholas got home,
there was a note on his door.

Dear Santa Duck,

Thank you so much for your help!
I couldn't have done it without you.
May I count on you again next year?

Gratefully, Santa

Nicholas felt so proud,
he forgot all about his list.
Getting to help Santa
was the best gift he
could ever get.

Well, almost . . .